Dear mouse friends,
Welcome to the world of

Geronimo Stilton

THE RODENT'S GAZETTE
EDITORIAL STAFF

Geronimo Stilton
A learned and brainy
mouse; editor of
The Rodent's Gazette

Thea Stilton
Geronimo's sister and
special correspondent at
The Rodent's Gazette

Trap Stilton
An awful joker;
Geronimo's cousin and
owner of the store
Cheap Junk for Less

Benjamin Stilton
A sweet and loving
nine-year-old mouse;
Geronimo's favorite
nephew

Geronimo Stilton

THE KARATE MOUSE

Scholastic Inc.

New York   Toronto   London   Auckland
Sydney   Mexico City   New Delhi   Hong Kong

ISBN: 978-0-545-10369-5

Text by Geronimo Stilton
Original title *Te Lo Do Io Il Karate!*
Cover by Giuseppe Ferrario
Illustrations by Federico Brusco, Valentina Grassini, and Chiara Sacchi

Special thanks to Beth Dunfey
Special thanks to Lidia Morson Tramontozzi
Special thanks to Al and Alison DiGrazia at the Midwood Martial Arts Center
Interior design by Kay Petronio

12 11 10 9 8 7 6 5 4 3   10 11 12 13 14 15/0

Printed in the U.S.A.   40
First printing, January 2010

HI, GERONIMO!

It was a nice, *quiet* spring morning. The sun was shining, and the birds were singing. I woke up feeling cheerful. I decided to treat myself to a nice, *relaxing* bubble bath. So I grabbed my favorite bath gel, Mr. Cheddar, and hopped right into the tub.

Oh, excuse me! Here I am telling you about my personal habits and I haven't even introduced myself. My name is Stilton, *Geronimo Stilton*. I'm the publisher of *The Rodent's Gazette*, the most famouse newspaper on Mouse Island.

As I was saying, I was in the tub enjoying some marvelously cheese-scented  bubble bath. I was right in the middle of shampooing my fur when the phone **RANG**.

I sighed. *Wasn't this supposed to be a nice, quiet day?*

I tried to climb out of the tub, but I couldn't see a thing — I had soap all over my eyes. But the phone kept ringing and ringing!

I put down my paw on the edge of the tub,

I PUT DOWN MY PAW...

...SLIPPED ON THE EDGE OF THE TUB...

slipped . . . and **dived** headfirst into the sink! The soap made the sink so slippery, I slid out and smashed against the bathroom door. Ouch! My snout was completely squished!

Wasn't this supposed to be a nice, quiet day?

I answered the phone with one paw and rubbed my bruised snout with the other. "Hello, *Geronimo Stilton* here. Or at least what's left of me!"

"Hi, Geronimo! This is **Hyena**, Bruce Hyena! Are you ready? I can't hear you. I asked: ARE YOU READY??"

...DIVED HEADFIRST INTO THE SINK...

...AND SMASHED MY SNOUT AGAINST THE DOOR!

are you ready?

Oh, no, not Bruce Hyena! Do you remember him? He's a devoted sportsmouse. He likes all kinds of athletic activity, especially extreme sports. And as you know, I am more of a bookmouse than a sportsmouse. But that doesn't stop Bruce from dragging me around on his adventures!*

Wasn't this supposed to be a nice, quiet day?

"Hmm, that depends on what you mean by 'ready,'" I replied cautiously. "**READY FOR WHAT?**"

w-w-warn me?

Bruce just laughed. "Didn't Shorty Tao warn you?"

"W-w-w-warn me about what?" I stammered.

Bruce started squeaking so fast, I could hardly keep up.

*If you want to read about my last adventure with Bruce, check out my bestseller, *The Race Across America.*

PERSONAL PROFILE

Name: Shorty Tao

Who she is: By day, she's the managing editor of *The Rodent's Gazette*; on weekends and at night, she's a karate world champion! She keeps trying to convince me to publish a karate handbook.

Interesting facts: She's Bruce Hyena's cousin. She's as tough as a rock, but melts like butter at the mention of her little brother, Baby Tao.

Favorite sports: Karate and triathlons

Annoying habits: She likes to pinch rodents to wake them up. In my case, she uses her pinch to stop me from panicking.

Believes in: Friendship, truth, and strength of character

Her passion: To do everything . . . enthusiastically!

Her motto: Laugh, laugh, laugh!

Her secret: Shorty Tao takes life lightly. She likes to tell jokes to cheer everyone up.

 These characters mean *"Shorty Tao"*

"That's bad, really bad!" he said. "So what you're telling me is that you're not in **shape**! You haven't trained! Your muscles are as squishy as string cheese! Well, too bad for you, Cheesehead! I'll pick you up tomorrow morning at five A.M. sharp! You'd better be waiting for me outside your mouse hole! Leave everything to me! Wait until you discover the fun adventure that's in store for you!"

I cried out in panic, "I can't go on a new adventure! I don't want to! **BRUUUUUUUUUUUCE!**"

But he had already hung up.

I was a goner! I was doomed! I was dead meat! I just couldn't let Bruce and Shorty drag me off on another adventure.

Wasn't this supposed to be a nice, quiet day???

A NIGHTMARISH NIGHT!

That night, I didn't sleep **A WINK**.

I was panic-stricken at the thought of Bruce's adventure. What had he gotten me into this time? My head was spinning with terrifying ideas.

Maybe Bruce was going to whisk me off to **BORNEO**, where it's one hundred degrees! I can't stand heat and humidity.

Maybe he was going to drag me to the **North Pole**, where it's fifty degrees **below zero**! I just hate the freezing cold.

Maybe Bruce was going to take me on safari deep in

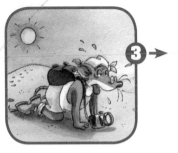

the **MOUSEHARA DESERT**! I absolutely cannot stand getting a sunburn.

I was so worried, I couldn't fall asleep. So I got up and fixed myself a nice cup of hot cheddar. Maybe that would relax me.

I sipped one cup, but nothing happened. I was still wide-awake.

I drank another cup: nothing.

I downed a **third** cup: nothing. So I had a fourth and then a **fifth**. Finally, I began to feel a LITTLE TINGLING in my paws.

After the twelfth cup, I fell dead asleep. *Snore!*

Unfortunately, by then it was 4:45 A.M.

Five minutes later, my **ALARM CLOCK** went off.

RING-RING!

My head felt as heavy as a block of Brie.
Slowly, I dragged myself out the door.
Bruce was waiting for me.

I FORGOT TO DO SOMETHING . . .

"Hey there, **CHEESEHEAD**! You ready? Huh? I can't hear you. I asked: ARE YOU READY?"

Before I could squeak, Bruce cut me off. "Oh, I get it. You're not saying anything because you feel **guilty** about being out of shape! Well, no worries. I've thought of everything. Looky here. I brought a couple of exercise charts."

I opened my mouth again, but I could hardly get a squeak in edgewise! "What?" Bruce cried. "Aren't you the least bit thankful? From now on, I'll be **CPT**!"

"CPT?" I asked nervously.

"**'CHEESEHEAD'S PERSONAL TRAINER'**!"

I felt awful. I was so tired, I could hardly talk or walk. But Bruce didn't seem to notice.

EXERCISE CHART

50-POUND DUMBBELLS

Lift over head
500 times

TRACTION

Pull-ups on bar
1,000 times

SPINNING

8 hours
a day

JUMP ROPE

30,000 jumps
a day

100-POUND WEIGHTS

Lift 50
times

RUNNING

25 miles
a day

PUSH-UPS

1,000 sets of 3

... AND DON'T TRY TO CHEAT!
—BRUCE!

He just yanked me into his Jeep.

I didn't have the **strength** to ask where we were headed.

"Okay, Cheesehead, tell me the truth. You're so excited about going, you can't find the words to thank me, right?" Bruce said.

I nodded wordlessly.

We started off. But after a couple of feet, Bruce STOPPED ABRUPTLY.

"Wh-wh-what's wrong?" I stammered.

"We have to make a quick stop at my office. I forgot to do something **ve-ry im-por-t-ant**!!!!"

"Did you forget to turn off the **wateR** faucet?" I asked.

"No, it's something really important!"

WATER?

GAS?

BURGLAR ALARM?

"Did you forget to turn off the **gas**?"

"No, no. It's really, really important!"

"I've got it! You forgot to turn on the **BURGLAR ALARM**!"

"No, no, no . . ." Bruce sighed. "I forgot to do my ten times ten. If you want to be a well-toned musclemouse like me, you have to stick to a routine, Cheesehead!"

So we went to his office, and Bruce did an entire series of **10 x 10**. That means lifting 200-pound barbells one hundred times.

As for me, I took a little ratnap. I needed all the rest I could get!

SHORTY TAO
IS THE TRAINER!

After he finished his exercises, Bruce and I went to pick up **Shorty Tao**. She was wearing a tracksuit and carrying a duffel bag that was bigger than she was! How could such a tiny little mouse be so **STRONG**?

Bruce winked at me. "Hey, Cheesehead, isn't my cousin in great shape? Ever since we were mouselings, our motto's been:

Shorty Tao

SHORTY TAO IS THE TRAINER,
BRUCE HYENA IS THE CHAMPION!"

Shorty is the trainer? Did that mean they were training me for something? But what? I had a **bad feeling** about this.

Bruce gave my tail an affectionate tug. "You're lucky to know us, Cheesehead!"

As soon as Shorty hopped into the Jeep, she gave Bruce the thumbs-up sign.

WHY? What were they up to? I was afraid to find out!

We zoomed away. About ten minutes later, we arrived at the airport. Bruce and Shorty went to check in by themselves. They kept whispering to each other. Every so often, one of them would glance over and wink at me.

BUT WHY? Why?? My whiskers were knotted with worry.

When it was time to go to the boarding gate, they blindfolded me.

BUT WHY, OH WHY? My tail was tingling with dread and anticipation!

Only after we boarded the plane and Bruce had strapped me into my seat, did they remove the **blindfold**.

"CLICK! Your belt's buckled! You can't escape now!" Bruce chuckled. "But don't worry. As usual, your old friend Bruce has everything taken care of! That's why I'm

CPT!" Then he turned to Shorty, and they continued their secret powwow.

While I tried (unsuccessfully) to relax, I caught a couple of words.

"Squeak . . . Squeak . . . organized . . . Squeak . . . training?"

TRAINING? So they *were* going to train me for something! But what??

"Squeak . . . did you sign him up?"

Sign me up?! For what? I didn't like the sound of that!

"Above all . . . Squeak . . . do you think he'll make it?"

MAKE IT? MAKE WHAT?! Where were they taking me?

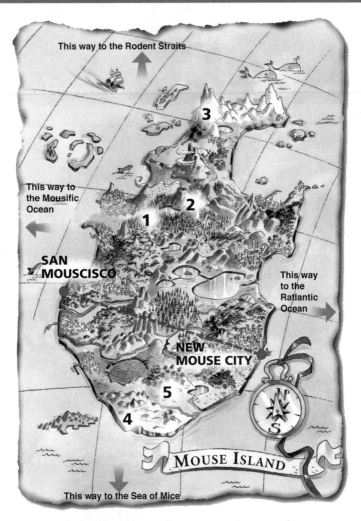

This way to the Rodent Straits

This way to the Mousific Ocean

3

2

1

SAN MOUSCISCO

This way to the Ratlantic Ocean

NEW MOUSE CITY

5

4

This way to the Sea of Mice

MOUSE ISLAND

1. Brimstone Lake
2. Roastedrat Volcano
3. Frozen Fur Peak
4. Mousehara Desert
5. Rio Mosquito

San Mouscisco is on the western coast of Mouse Island. It looks out on Stray Cat Harbor, famouse for the enormouse and voracious cats who once lived there.

- - - - - FLIGHT PATH FROM NEW MOUSE CITY TO SAN MOUSCISCO

I HAD TO DO
SOMETHING!

After a long flight, we finally *LANDED*.

"Hey, **Cheesehead**, we're here!" exclaimed Bruce. "Are you hungry? I could eat a cat! Why don't we get a **GIGANTIC PIZZA**? Good idea, right?"

Food was the last thing on my mind. Where was I? Where had they taken me?

A GIGANTIC PIZZA

A feeling of uneasiness began to settle in my stomach. The uneasiness quickly turned into gnawing WOrry. Then the gnawing worry became outright ANXIETY. And finally, the moment came to **PAAAANIC!!!**

That was it. I'd had it! Nothing was going

THE TEN STAGES

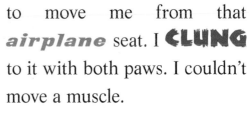

FAKE CALMNESS

UNEASINESS

to move me from that *airplane* seat. I **CLUNG** to it with both paws. I couldn't move a muscle.

Bruce and Shorty tried everything they could think of to convince me to get up.

"Come on, Geronimo!" Shorty cajoled me. "Don't make cheesecake out of a cheese crumb. You'll see it's no big deal."

Bruce shook his snout sadly. "I expected better from you, **CHAMP**. Look around!

NERVOUSNESS

WORRY

ANXIETY

OF PANIC

Everyone's staring at you. Where did you leave your pride, huh?"

"In New Mouse City!" I shouted.

Bruce was right. Everyone *was* staring at me. And I couldn't blame them. It wasn't every day you saw *Geronimo Stilton*, a bestselling author and publisher, act like such a nincompoop!

But there was nothing I could do. **IT WAS BIGGER THAN ME!**

Have you ever panicked? Trust me, it's a horrid feeling! You can't control yourself. You're not

PANIC!!! 10

ALARM 9

HYSTERICAL LAUGHTER 8

HEART PALPITATIONS 6

ANGUISH 7

Pinccch!!!!

in charge. It's weird.

Pinccch!!!!

Suddenly, I felt a sharp pain on my neck. "Ouch! Wh-what was that?!"

That was Shorty Tao's famouse **pinch**. "I'm sorry, Geronimo," she said earnestly. "I had to do something to help you snap out of it. So I pinched you. Don't you feel better now?"

I took a deep breath. "I-I-I-I guess so. Thank you, Shorty! I-I-I'm a little better."

But before I could finish squeaking,  *I FAINTED!*

THE KARATE WORLD CHAMPIONSHIP?

"Geronimo! Geronimo! Are you okay?"

I could hear Shorty's squeak. It sounded as if she were far, far, far *awaaaaay*.

I shook my snout, trying to wake up. "Wh-wh-where am I?" I mumbled.

"You're in San Mouscisco," she answered. "Bruce and I brought you here."

Slowly, I opened my eyes. First I saw **SHORTY**, then Bruce. He gave me the **OK** sign. Smiling *stupidly*, I returned it.

Suddenly, Shorty's words sank in. I sat up. "Wait a second! What am I doing in San Mouscisco?"

Shorty looked at Bruce, who shrugged.

Bruce's Paw

"Geronimo, it's time we told you," she said. "You're here to enter a tournament. In a week, you'll compete in the **karate world championship** that will be held here in San Mouscisco. I'll be entering, too! You have seven days to learn all there is to know about karate."

I stared at her, **dumbfounded**.

"What do you think?" she asked me anxiously.

I didn't know what to say. So **I fainted again**!

BUT I'M A TOTAL KLUTZ!

When I finally came to, I was in a hotel. I'd been out so long, I'd completely missed the trip from the airport.

"Oh, good! You're awake again," Shorty said cheerfully. "OK, get yourself cleaned up. We'll meet in the lobby in half an hour, and then we'll head over to the **dojo**.* Your first round of **INTENSE TRAINING** is about to begin."

With that, Shorty opened up her huge duffel bag and removed a tiny backpack. She pawed it to me. "Here's everything you'll need: your federation badge, your belt, and your **gi**. That's the white karate uniform."

As we scampered to our room, Bruce put

---

* Karate began in Japan, so many of the words used in the sport are Japanese. A *dojo* is a school for learning karate.

BADGE

GI AND BELT

his paw around me. "So, **Cheesehead**, what do you have to say for yourself? Aren't you **excited** about the surprise we gave you? I mean, think about it. This is probably your only chance to compete in the **karate world championship**! Aren't you a tiny bit grateful?"

"How can I be grateful?" I protested. "Bruce, you know me! I'm a total klutz!"

He slapped my back so hard, I almost toppled over. "**CHAMP, LET'S DO IT** for Shorty Tao! Get washed up and then we'll begin your training."

Reluctantly, I did as he said. What choice did I have? I was trapped thousands of miles from home with two fitness fanatics! Oh why, oh why, did I have such crazy friends?

Half an hour later, the three of us met in the hotel lobby. Then we HOPPED on the bus to the *dojo* for my FIRST TRAINING SESSION.

I'M REALLY MORE OF A BOOKMOUSE . . .

Once we arrived at the *dojo*, I scurried into the locker room and got changed. I was doing fine until I tried putting on the *gi*. I had no idea how to tie my belt, which was a little humiliating. Luckily, Shorty Tao came to my rescue.

We went out onto the **tatami**, which were the rubber mats covering the floor, and began to get WARMED UP.

Bruce was sitting in the bleachers. "GO, CHEESEHEAD, GO!" he shouted. "Remember, you need to concentrate! FOCUS! YOU CAN DO IT! Now get out there, and show us your stuff!"

I WAS SO EMBARRASSED!

I should've been used to it, but I wasn't. You see, when you're with Bruce, you're always the center of attention. That's hard for a quiet, shy bookmouse like me.

Shorty introduced me to our world-famous **sensei**,* MOUSESHIRO YAMAMOUSE.

"Are you the new martial arts athlete?" *Sensei* Yamamouse asked. "That's strange. You don't look very **tough**!"

"Well, I'm really more

*Sensei is the Japanese word for teacher.

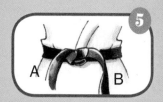

of a bookmouse, *Sensei*. . . ." I began.

"Who said you could interrupt me?" *Sensei* Yamamouse snapped. "If it happens again, you'll be jumping rope for thirty minutes!"

I gulped. Unlike me, this rodent *was* very **TOUGH**!

"Now, as I was squeaking before I was so rudely interrupted, you don't look very tough. But I trust Shorty Tao. If she says you're ready, then you're ready."

Sensei Yamamouse

We began the **TRAINING**. I kept my eyes glued on Shorty and tried to imitate her movements. She was really excellent. Every move she made was *fluid* and *graceful*. She didn't look like she was doing karate. It looked more like dancing!

"Geronimo, you can't wear glasses when you're training!" yelled *Sensei* Yamamouse.

"Well, I'm such a bookmouse that I really need glasses to see, *Sensei*. . . ."

"Who said you could interrupt me?" *Sensei* Yamamouse said. "If it happens again, you'll climb the rope fifty times!"

We continued TRAINING for FOUR solid hours! *Sensei* Yamamouse spat out one command after another, and we tried to execute them faithfully.

After two hours, I raised my paw and asked if I could have a drink of water.

"Who said you could INTERRUPT me? And who said you could drink during a lesson? Don't you know it's **FORBIDDEN**? Now, drop and do one hundred push-ups. No, make it two hundred. That'll make you stronger!"

I did as he said. What choice did I have? I was too terrified to disobey!

When i finished, i felt like a dead mouse!

A VERY
SERIOUS KNOT

three seconds!

In just...

...three seconds...

...I was ready!

The next morning, I was sound asleep. My body ached from the tip of my snout to the tip of my tail. I needed rest! But Shorty Tao had other plans. "Geronimo, get up!" she squeaked. "You have an appointment with the massage mouse!"

I fumbled for my glasses. "BUT IT'S FIVE O'CLOCK IN THE MORNING!"

"That's right, and you're already late!" she replied. "We'll have **BREAKFAST** at seven and then we'll head back to the *dojo*. Now, are you getting up by yourself, or should I pinch you?"

In three seconds flat, I was up, showered, and ready to go.

"Good for you, Geronimo!" said Shorty. "Now go to Room 217. The massage mouse is waiting for you."

HaNS MuSCLeturNeR

I was a little APPREHENSIVE. But it was a massage. How bad could it be?

So I went to Room 217. A **massive** mouse dressed in WHITE opened the door.

"You must be Geronimo," he said curtly. "I'm **HANS MUSCLETURNER**. Please lie down on the table."

HANS MUSCLETURNER'S EXPRESSIONS

HAPPY

SAD

CONFUSED

OVERJOYED

ANGRY

FRUSTRATED

ANNOYED

SATISFIED

SCARED

I lay down, but I wasn't at all **RELAXED**. Holey cheese, how could I relax when a mouse the size of a truck was about to crunch my bones?

Hans took some oil from a little bottle and rubbed it all over his paws. Then he began to massage my back.

"Geronimo, your muscles are **VERY TENSE**," he said. "I have to dig my paws into them!" ·········

"I guess if you really have to . . ." I replied nervously.

He was **HURTING** me a little, but I must say I was beginning to feel better.

"Hmm . . . here's a **VERY SERIOUS** knot," he said. "I have to dig my elbow into it." ·················

"Your elbow? Well, all right, if you really have to."

Hans planted his elbow between my ribs. It hurt a little more than his paws, but it did seem to be helping.

After a while, he stopped. "Here's a knot that's **VERY, VERY SERIOUS**," he said. "This one, we'll treat differently."

"OK," I responded calmly. "What do you mean, 'differently'?"

"**Trust me!**" Hans said.

Before I knew what was happening, he had climbed onto the table. He began walking up and down my back!

"Take a deep breath," he instructed me. Then he stomped his heel into my shoulder!

"OUUCCCCHHH!" I shrieked.

"Done!" **HANS** cried triumphantly. "How do you feel?"

"**I WANT TO GO TO THE HOSPITAL!!!!!!!!**" I shrieked.

KARATE = RESPECT

Training was **very hard**.

Sensei Yamamouse was very strict with me. But soon, with help from him and Shorty Tao, I started to improve.

First of all, I felt a lot more in shape. My muscles didn't ache as much. And my ability to **concentrate** had changed. I discovered that karate has a lot more to do with the head than with the muscles.

I had learned quite a bit of _kata_, a series of punches and kicks in the air against an imaginary opponent. **Kata** really helped me try different combinations of moves, steps, and turns.

In addition, Shorty was teaching me a lot about the spirit and philosophy of karate. "Many mice think karate is a violent **martial** art. But it's not. Karate teaches us to control ourselves and to respect our opponents. It also teaches us loyalty and truth."

I was puzzled. "Really? Respect, loyalty, and truth?" I asked. "I don't understand."

Shorty nodded. "Think of it this way. Imagine yourself in front of an opponent. What's the first thing you do?"

Well, that was an easy question. "**I get scared!**" I answered.

Shorty started laughing. "No, Geronimo! The first thing you do is **bow**. That bow

shows your respect and gratitude. It says, 'THIS MATCH WILL HELP ME LEARN AND GROW, AND

I'LL HELP YOU LEARN AND GROW, TOO.' Karate teaches kindness and respect.

"On the tatami, everyone is himself or herself," Shorty continued. "There's no cheating in karate: Everyone appears as he or she really is. You can't hide your flaws. *Karate encourages us to be sincere and honest!*"

Shorty was right. There was much more to karate than I'd realized at first. The art of karate (yes, karate is a true art) was really beginning to grow on me.

Shorty looked at me gravely. "Geronimo, karate is the perfect sport for a brainy mouse like you. It brings together the **heart**, the head, and the body. Think about what you've learned today. We repeat the philosophy of karate when we kneel and bid farewell at the end of every training session. We call these rules the *dojo kun*."

DOJO KUN

Dojo is the Japanese word for "training place." *Kun* means "rules." At the end of every lesson, the *dojo kun* is recited. At some dojos, the *dojo kun* is posted outside the door. Anyone who practices karate must try to obey the *dojo kun*, whether inside or outside of the *dojo*.

DOJO ETIQUETTE

Whenever you enter or leave a *dojo*, you *rei* (bow). At the beginning and end of class, you *rei*. You *rei* to the *sensei*, you *rei* to the teachers of the past, you *rei* to your training partner, you *rei* to your opponent. The *rei* is a sign of respect.

There are two types of bows in karate: one standing up and one kneeling. For the standing rei:
1. *Put your feet together, with your hands at your sides. Look straight ahead.*
2. *Bend forward from the waist, looking ahead. Say, "Osu!"*

HITOTSU: JINKAKU KANSEI NI TSUTOMURU KOTO.
First: Strive to perfect your character.

HITOTSU: MAKOTO NO MICHI O MAMORU KOTO.
First: Be faithful and protect the way of truth.

HITOTSU: DORYOKU NO SEISHIN O YASHINAU KOTO.
First: Try your hardest.

HITOTSU: REIGI O OMONZURU KOTO.
First: Respect one another.

HITOTSU: KEKKI NO YU O IMASHIMURU KOTO
First: Refrain from violent behavior.

This is the Japanese character for *hitotsu*, which means "first." It is said before every rule to show that they are all equally important.

I'll Help You!

The day I'd dreaded was finally here. It was the night before the tournament.

I'd expected to be incredibly nervous, and I was. But I was also incredibly excited! Of course, I had done everything I could to prepare. I had learned enough to advance to a green belt! And I had also perfected a **TOP-SECRET** move!

After dinner, Shorty knocked at my door.

"Here, Geronimo, this is your number," she told me as she handed me a piece of paper. "Put it on the back of your *gi* jacket. You have to sew it on!"

Geronimo's number

I didn't know how to tell Shorty this, but I didn't know how to **sew**!

The rest of the team from Mouse Island began to arrive. Everyone held a *gi* jacket and a number in his or her paws. They all had the same embarrassed look on their snouts.

Shorty took one look at them and immediately understood. "Okay, rodents! I have a needle and enough thread for everyone. I'll help you!"

Then Shorty called her two best friends from the team, **Daniella** and **Miyagi**, who came with reinforcements. **THE NEXT THING I KNEW**, my room was transformed into a sewing factory!

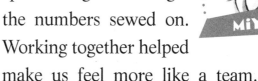

Miyagi

Everyone pulled together to get the numbers sewed on. Working together helped make us feel more like a team. And being in such good company helped me forget my nerves.

Daniella

BREAKFAST OF CHAMPIONS

I couldn't eat anything for breakfast. I was way too nervous.

As for Shorty Tao, Daniella, and Miyagi, they ate a **HUGE** breakfast. I don't know how they did it. My stomach was in *knots* even an expert sailmouse couldn't untie.

Bruce scampered over to our table and slapped me on the back so hard, I almost fell out of my chair.

"Hey, Geronimo!" he said. "You look

AN ATHLETE'S BREAKFAST
Around two hours before every practice or competition, it's a good idea to have a healthy breakfast rich in complex carbohydrates. Go for whole-grain toast or cereal, low-fat milk or yogurt, and some fruit.

terrible! Is it nerves? I know what a scaredy mouse you can be."

Bruce knew me too well! I **WAS TERRIFIED** about performing my karate moves in front of the whole team, plus a judge and an audience. But did he have to bring it up in front of my teammates?

"*Pssst! Please lower your squeak!*" I pleaded with him.

"**DON'T FEEL EMBARRASSED**, Cheesehead!" Bruce practically shouted. "Everyone gets paralyzed by fear sometimes! I mean, *I* don't, of course, but the average bookmouse like you is a different story."

Now everyone was looking at me! Why, oh why did Bruce have such a **loud** squeak?! Fortunately, Daniella and Miyagi were giving me their kindest smiles. Shyly, I smiled back at them.

Shorty took my paw. "Don't listen to him, Geronimo!" she whispered. "I have faith in you!"

At **SEVEN O'CLOCK** on the dot, the bus came to pick us up. Half an hour later, we pulled up at San Mouscisco's **biggest sports arena**. The whole team scurried to the locker room to change. Something about putting on my *gi* made the reality of what was about to happen sink in. My tail was trembling, my heart was beating like crazy, my mouth was dry, and my paws were drenched with **SWEAT**.

On top of everything else, my **EYES** started to bulge. I hardly looked like a mouse anymore — I looked more like a fish who's just discovered that he's on the menu for dinner.

HOLEY CHEESE, what was happening to me? Suddenly, I wasn't able to move a step.

I was having a panic attack. It was sheer
FEAR! And I was completely paralyzed.

Shorty scampered over to me.

"Okay, Geronimo!" she said confidently.
"It's time to go out to the **tatami**."

I couldn't answer.

"Didn't you hear me, Geronimo?" she
asked. "Move those paws!"

I still couldn't answer. I just stared straight
ahead, like a **ZOMBIE**.

"Geronimo, I'm telling you for the last time.
Either move or I'll . . ."

She grabbed my neck and . . .

Oh, no! She had given
me her dreaded **pinch**!

Her method did the
trick. The pain was
so overwhelming, I
snapped right out of it.

Pinnch!!!!

THE KOKORO

The stands that surrounded the *tatami* were packed. I don't think I've ever seen so many rodents in one place, not even at the Bruce Ratsteen concert my sister, Thea, dragged me to last year. The place was buzzing with EXCITEMENT.

Athletes from all over the world filled the *tatami.* Everyone was busy **warming up**.

As I looked around in awe, Shorty Tao came up behind me. Instinctively, I **stepped away** from her. I wasn't about to risk another **pinch**.

"Relax, Geronimo!" she squeaked reassuringly. "I can tell you're really nervous.

SIDE THRUST KICK

That's normal. Everyone gets nervous before their first tournament."

"Of course I'm nervous!" I cried. "I'm afraid I'll get hurt!"

Shorty LOOKED at me closely. There was a shrewd expression on her snout. "Geronimo, is that the only thing bothering you?"

STRETCHING

ACTUALLY, now that she mentioned it, there *was* something else. I hadn't thought about it too much because, well, I was afraid to think about it. But I was

STEPPING PUNCH

absolutely terrified of failing! I didn't want to disappoint Shorty, Bruce, *sensei* **Yamamouse**, and the entire team. Everyone was counting on me, and I felt the enormouse **weight** of this responsibility.

Failing my teammates was without a doubt my biggest fear. (That, and the possibility that'd I'd need reconstructive surgery when I got back home!)

SHORTY TAO

"You're right, Shorty," I admitted. "There is something else. I'm afraid I'll be a huge disappointment to all of you."

Shorty smiled and gave me a hug. "Geronimo, it's natural to have butterflies in your stomach. This is your first competition, and it's a **WORLD** championship! But you've got to relax. Try to control your emotions! Visualize the meet, the tatami, the LIGHTS, the public, and what you'll feel when you meet your opponents. Then, when it's your turn, there won't be any SURPRISES."

I smiled at her. I was lucky to have such a good friend by my side. Her advice was excellent.

KOKORO
(heart)

"And, Geronimo, this is the most important thing." Shorty paused. "Remember to fight with your heart. The **KOKORO**, as the Japanese say."

"*Kokoro*?" I repeated. "What a beautiful word."

"If you do fight with your heart, and with truth and courage, everything will go smoothly," Shorty continued. "The **SECRET** is to always do your best. That's the only way you can meet every difficulty with confidence.

There's an old Japanese saying I think about before every match:

> "Karate is not about winning, it's about not losing!"

"Thank you, **SHORTY!**" I said, giving her a big hug. I already felt a lot better. Her words had given me courage.

First, I would try to visualize the competition. Concentrate on my heart, my kokoro. Then I would

GERONIMO STILTON, GET READY!

It was time for the opening ceremony. All the athletes paraded into the stadium, waving their country's flags. The mice in the stands applauded them. Then it was time for the competition to begin.

The loudsqueaker blasted, **"GERONIMO STILTON, GET READY ON THE TATAMI!"**

Shorty Tao squeezed my paw. "I know you're ready for this, Geronimo. Remember to concentrate on your *kokoro*."

I gave her paw a squeeze, then approached the *tatami*. But just as I was about to step out, my paw got stuck between the mats.

"SECOND CALL FOR GERONIMO STILTON!"
the loudsqueaker blared.

Uh-oh! I tried yanking my paw out. I
pulled it every which way. But my paw just
wouldn't move. It was as if I were caught in
a mousetrap — ouch!

"Come on, Geronimo!" I heard SHORTY
yell. "You'll be eliminated after the third
call!"

I pulled and pushed and heaved as hard

as I could, but **nothing** happened. I couldn't get unstuck!

"GERONIMO STILTON, THIS IS YOUR THIRD AND FINAL CALL!" the loudsqueaker boomed.

I was near tears. Was it possible I would lose the championship because of a trapped paw?

Just when I was about to give up . . .

POP!

My paw popped out of the mat! I scurried over to the *tatami* as quickly as I could.

Argh!

Go, Cheesehead, Go!

I stepped onto the **tatami**. Immediately, a tomblike silence fell over the stadium. Every eye was on me, Geronimo Stilton, a mouse who had known nothing about karate just one week ago! I tried not to let it get to me.

MOUSOSHI CHAMPRAT

On the opposite side of the *tatami*, my opponent stepped out. It was Mousoshi Champrat.

He was a very **TOUGH-LOOKING** mouse!

A wave of nausea crashed over me. I could feel my fur turning green. Then I thought of Shorty Tao's words: *The secret is to always do your best.*

The silence was mounting. It was a VERY, VERY, VERY TENSE moment. Then . . .

WOO-HOOOOOOOOOOOOOOOOOOOOO!

Startled, I looked up at the stands. Bruce was sitting in the front row, blasting on a plastic trumpet.

"You can do it, Cheesehead!" he shouted. "Show him what you're made of!" He waved a big banner in the air.

GO, CHEESEHEAD, GO!

I WAS MORTIFIED! But I wasn't surprised. Things like this happen when you have a friend like BRUCE.

The referee scampered over to me. "Excuse me. Are you Geronimo Stilton, or Cheesehead? Our roster shows this match is between Mousoshi Champrat and Geronimo Stilton."

"My name is Stilton, *Geronimo Stilton*!" I said with as much **confidence** as I could muster. "I'm ready!"

The referee walked away. He looked unconvinced. He whispered something to the judges. They all turned to look at me suspiciously.

I tried to put that out of my mind. At last, it was time for **MY FIRST MATCH**!

HIIIIII YAAAAA!

The crowd began clapping their paws and stamping the ground. They made so much noise, it seemed as if the **arena** would collapse!

Mousoshi Champrat and I began studying each other after we did our *rei*. We were each trying to figure out what kind of opponent the other was.

Then Champrat began a RAPID combination of attacks: **FIST, KICK, FIST, FIST!** It looked like a **MASSIVE** wall of muscles was coming right at me. I had no plan of counterattack, only *FLIGHT*! I began to race around the tatami, determined not to let Champrat catch up.

Run! Run! Run!

Champrat started to get annoyed. I swear I saw smoke come out of his nostrils. He looked angrier than a cat with a bad case of fleas!

Champrat tried to hit me with another combination of attacks: **SIDE KICK, FIST!**

But I was too fast for him. Champrat was **big**, tall, and covered with muscles, but he was a lot slower than I was!

I suddenly remembered my new secret move. It was time to use it! I began concentrating really hard. Then I started running even faster than before.

I concentrated...

...began to run...

As I picked up speed, I leaped into the air and made

Hiii yaa!!!

a powerful **jumping-front-reverse-roundhouse kick**.

This was an ancient and

extremely

secret move

SENSEI YAMAMOUSE

had taught me.

As I kicked, I yelled,

...and made a flying kick, losing my balance.

...leaped high...

"HIII YAAAA!!!*"

Suddenly, there was an explosion of blinding flashes.
I lost my balance and did a backward somersault.

*The yell gives the move more power.

5

I did a backward somersault.

I **LANDED** on Champrat, knocking him over.

There was moment of silence, then the crowd began to applaud like crazy.

I **STUMBLED** to my paws and began to massage my tail. Moldy mozzarella, that hurt! But Champrat was K.O.'d — that is, **KNOCKED OUT**!

I scurried over to help him. "Champrat, are you OK? Did I hurt you? I'm so sorry. I didn't do it on purpose! The flashes made me lose my balance!"

Champrat just looked up at me and said, "You're . . . you're . . . you're . . . amazing! I've never seen such a move! I'm honored to have lost to an athlete of such caliber and experience!"

The loudsqueaker announced, "GERONIMO STILTON IS THE WINNER OF THE WORLD CHAMPIONSHIP!"

Wait, what? What did they mean, "World Championship"?!

Shorty Tao and SENSEI YAMAMOUSE ran toward me with open paws.

"Geronimooooooo!!!! YOU WON!!! You're phenomenal!!!" Shorty squeaked.

"Did I really win?" I asked incredulously.

"Didn't you hear the announcement earlier?" SHORTY asked. "The Peruvian backed out because of a PULLED muscle, the Italian dislocated a knee, and the Chinese athlete slipped in the locker room, hit his head, and lost his memory. Poor thing, he couldn't remember a single karate move. So you and Champrat were the only ones in your event left, and you beat him!!!"

I was in shock! I hugged **SHORTY**.
The crowd kept on cheering. Bruce was
FRANTICALLY waving in the bleachers.
I waved back.

I couldn't believe it. I was the . . .

Wow!

Hi, Bruce!

...WORLD
CHAMPION!!

1,000 TAILS PROUDLY WAG

The competition continued. I was glad my match was so early in the day; now I could relax and enjoy the rest of the tournament. Many other athletes from Mouse Island performed well. Shorty, Daniella, and Miyagi all successfully defended their titles in the female **EVENTS**.

At the end of the day, it was time for the medal ceremony. The podium was **very high** and **brightly lit**.

All the athletes formed a line. I shook Champrat's paw. Then I heard the **loudsqueaker** announce the winners in my event.

"IN THIRD PLACE, FERDINAND MOUSCOS FROM THE PHILIPPINES!"

The athlete stepped onto the third step on the podium.

"IN SECOND PLACE, MOUSOSHI CHAMPRAT FROM JAPAN!"

Champrat took his place on the second step on the podium.

"AND IN FIRST PLACE, OUR NEW WORLD CHAMPION, GERONIMO STILTON FROM MOUSE ISLAND!"

I scampered up to my place on the highest step on the podium. I was very excited! The crowd was cheering and calling our names. The photographers were taking thousands of **P H O T O S**.

Gazing out at the stands I saw my *family*! My sister Thea, my cousin Trap, and my adorable nephew Benjamin were all beaming with pride as they cheered for me.

What a *fabumouse* surprise!

After the MEDALS were given, there was a moment of silence, and then Mouse Island's national anthem came over the loudsqueaker. It was **VERY MOVING**. I felt so proud to represent my country, Mouse Island!

Mouse Island's National Anthem

A thousand voices squeak as one,
A thousand tails proudly wag,
A thousand whiskers boldly quiver,
A thousand paws raise your yellow flag!
Under our fur, a thousand hearts beat for you,
Sweet, sweet Mouse Island.

When the anthem was over, I raised my arms and waved to all my fans.

From across the podium, Shorty Tao flashed me the thumbs-up sign. Grinning proudly, I returned it. Then I went to find my family.

My little nephew Benjamin jumped up to hug me. "Uncle Geronimo, you were **тнe ваsт**! I knew you could do it! You were totally awesome!"

My sister winked at me. "I'm so proud of you, Gerry Berry!"

Trap slapped me on the back. I braced myself for a mocking comment. (Teasing me is my cousin's favorite hobby.) "I've gotta tell you, Germeister, you did well!" he said. "That flying kick was *masterful*. I had no idea you were so athletic!"

I threw my paws around all three of them. Winning the tournament was wonderful, of course, but winning my *family's* pride was **way more**

THEA

TRAP

BENJAMIN

important. It's great to share your happiness with rodents who **love** you. I was one lucky mouse. At that moment, nothing could take away my *happiness*.

At least, that's what I thought.

I'M A VERY PRIVATE RODENT!

At that moment, two of the tournament's officials approached me. They both had **serious** looks on their snouts. "Mr. Stilton, please come this way."

I was **PUZZLED**. "R-r-r-right now?" I asked. "Where are we going? And why?"

"To the medical clinic," the first official replied. "We must go at once. We have to test you to make sure you didn't **CHEAT**."*

"But . . . but . . . why me?" I asked.

"It's nothing personal," the second official explained. "All contestants must submit to the test."

So I said a quick good-bye to my family and followed the officials. I was

---

*At the end of every competition, officials give the contestants a urine test. If an athlete is found to have used an illegal substance to improve his or her performance, he or she is disqualified.

worried, even though I knew I hadn't done anything wrong.

When we got to the clinic, a stern-looking nurse pawed me a plastic container. "Here you go," he said. "You know what to do."

But I didn't! "I'm sorry, but I don't understand."

"You have to urinate," he said patiently. "Then we'll test it to see if you cheated."

Of course, **I KNEW I HADN'T CHEATED**, but I still felt a little ashamed at having to

It was embarrassing!

take a test to prove it. Especially now that I knew I'd have to pee into a little cup! It was embarrassing. I'm a very private rodent!

I didn't think things could get **worse**, but they did. I'd just started toward the bathroom when **suddenly** I heard the nurse's voice behind me.

"I'm sorry, Mr. Stilton, but you can't go alone. One of the officials from the tournament will have to stand guard outside the door."

I was so surprised, I almost tripped over my own tail! "Wh-wh-wh-what? I'll never be able to go if there's a stranger right outside!" I answered desperately.

The nurse smiled kindly at me. "I'm so sorry, Mr. Stilton. I know it's terrible that a few CHEATERS have made these rules necessary. But these are the rules. If you don't follow them, we will have no choice but TO DISQUALIFY YOU."

I knew what I had to do. The honesty of my entire team was at stake. If I needed to pee in a cup to prove my integrity, **I'D DO IT, BY CHEESE**!

So I headed to the bathroom. An official followed me. He looked almost as embarrassed as I was.

"Um, could I have something to drink?" I mumbled. "A little water might help me."

Without a squeak, he pawed me a bottle of water. I drank it in one gulp. But it **didn't help**.

They brought me another bottle. I drank that one down even faster than the first. But

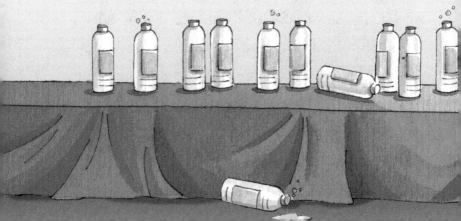

nothing happened. So I drank another, and then another, and then another. But still — **nothing**!

The official and the nurse were starting to look at me a little suspiciously. Finally, the official said, "Mr. Stilton, if there's something you want to tell us . . ." he trailed off.

The nurse nodded. "It would save everybody time (and water) if you'd **confess**."

"WHAT?" I cried. "NO! I HAVE NOTHING TO CONFESS! I'M JUST A LITTLE SELF-CONSCIOUS, THAT'S ALL."

The official gave me a sympathetic look. "We understand, Mr. Stilton. But we have

other athletes we must test. You really have to **HURRY UP.**"

I gulped. I tried to concentrate. I drank yet another bottle of water. And then suddenly, I really had to go!

I scampered into the stall and did my business. When I was done, I was so relieved. I gave the nurse my biggest smile as I pawed him my plastic container. He began my test at once.

Butch
Strongmouse

I sat down to wait. Another athlete came in. I recognized him immediately. It was **Butch Strongmouse**, the **biggest** and most muscular athlete. He looked *worried*.

Shorty Tao came

in next. She seemed **cheerful**. "Hiya, Geronimo!" she said, waving to me. She went into the ladies' room with a female official and came out with her container a few minutes later. She sat down next to me to wait.

After about fifteen minutes, the nurse gave us the results.

"Geronimo Stilton, your test is **negative**," the nurse said. "You may go!"

I smiled. I knew my test would be fine, of course, but I hadn't realized until that moment how **tense** I had been!

The nurse consulted his list. "Shorty Tao, you're clean. But Butch Strongmouse, I'm sorry to say that your test was positive. You're **DISQUALIFIED!**"

Butch burst out crying. "**waaH!** My trainer told me I should take something to make me stronger . . . **Sniff, Sniff**. He said they were

almost the same as **vitamins**. I didn't want to, but he told me it was the only way I could win!"

Shorty patted Butch on the back. "Your trainer was **wrong**! That stuff is illegal, and it can be very dangerous to your health. Plus, it goes against the TRUE SPIRIT of karate. If you had won the championship, what satisfaction would you have had? Butch, you can't ever win by cheating!"

Butch just cried harder. "You're right!" he blubbered. "I was an *idiot*!"

"You're not an idiot," I told him. "You just made a mistake. But remember, there's always next time."

"That's right!" said Shorty. "Keep on

training, and I bet you'll do well next time — without using anything you shouldn't."

At that, Butch dried his eyes. "You're right!" he shouted. "I promise I'll never do it again. I'll respect myself and the true spirit of karate! Thank you, my friends!"

Shorty Tao and I hugged Butch. Then we left the clinic together.

As we headed toward the bus, BRUCE approached us. Uh-oh! He probably had another embarrassing trick up his tail. I looked around, but there was no place to hide. So I steeled myself.

Imagine my surprise when he hugged me! "Well done, Cheesehead!" Bruce said. "I'M really proud of you!"

That's Bruce for you! He might be embarrassing sometimes, but at heart, he's a great friend!

SAYONARA!

That night, there was a party for all the karate competitors. It was called the *SAYONARA PARTY*. (*Sayonara* means "good-bye" in Japanese.) All my new teammates were there, plus Shorty, Miyagi, Daniella, *Sensei* Yamamouse, Bruce, and even my *family*.

It was **so much fun**!

Many of the mice spoke different languages, but we understood one another anyway. We were living proof that **SPORTS UNITE EVERYONE**!

At the end of the party, we said our good-byes. With tears in our eyes, we promised to keep in touch.

AN INTERESTING IDEA

The next day, we took a plane back to New Mouse City. When we landed, we had a big surprise: The mayor was there to greet us! There was a parade in our honor.

Everyone was there to celebrate: *Sensei* Yamamouse, Daniella, Miyagi, Shorty, and **BRUCE**. I hugged my teammates with pride.

Finally, it was time to return to *The Rodent's*

Gazette. I was sure to be tail-deep in work after a week off!

When I got in, I discovered the staff was all waiting for me. As soon as I scurried in the door wearing my championship **medal**, they burst into *applause*.

Even Shorty Tao was there. She had brought her little brother, Baby Tao, who was already promising to be a karate champion.

After the *festivities* were over, Shorty sidled over to me and whispered, "Geronimo, I have an interesting idea for you."

DESTINATION: OKINAWA!

Want to know what Shorty Tao squeaked?

She asked me to take another trip with her and Bruce Hyena. Destination: OKINAWA, Japan. That's right! Okinawa, the island where KARATE was born!

I was so thrilled to learn more about this ancient martial art, that I accepted!

SHORTY TAO
age eight

Now, you know I don't like to travel. But I was so excited, I hardly noticed how many hours we were on the plane! (And believe me, it was a lot of hours.)

SHORTY told me many stories about her childhood, including

tales about how she started to learn **KARATE**, and how karate had helped her in many situations.

Thanks to karate, she had become a strong, determined mouse. Karate had helped her reach many of her **goals**.

SHORTY TAO
at her college graduation

As I listened to Shorty, I realized that karate had also helped me! The concentration I'd learned assisted me with my fears and shyness. Thanks to karate, I had learned that a mouse can do **anything** he or she wants, as long as he or she is willing to work at it.

Once we reached **OKINAWA**, we had our work cut out for us.

SHORTY TAO
World Champion

THE DOJO

BRUCE, SHORTY AND GERONIMO IN KIMONOS

TEA CEREMONY —TOO HOT!

We were determined to discover the origins of karate and learn as much as we could about **Japanese** culture. It was the perfect project for a bookmouse like me.

I was so excited! Could I do it? Would I be able to learn the ancient rules of the **SAMURAI**?

That, dear rodent friends, is a story for another book.

But I will tell you about it someday. I give you my word. The word of *Geronimo Stilton!*

THE ABC'S OF KARATE

BELT

The color of a karate student's belt represents his or her rank, ranging from white to black. The ranks below black belt are called *kyu* grades. They often go in the following order: white, yellow, orange, green, purple, and brown. The ranks of black belt and above are called *dan* grades. To progress from one color belt to the next, the student must pass a test. During competitions, athletes often wear red or blue belts.

GERI

Kicking. In karate, it is possible to do front, circular, side, crescent, and back kicks.

Front kick

Side-thrust kick

DOJO

The place where karate is taught and practiced. The word *dojo* also means a place where one's body and spirit are strengthened.

GI

The karate training uniform: white pants and jacket tied with a belt. The *gi* dates back to 1922, to the first public karate demonstration in Tokyo. Before then, training was done in everyday clothing or shorts, depending on the climate.

KARATE

Karate literally means "empty hand." (*Kara = empty; te = hand.*) Karate is a technique that makes it possible to defend oneself using only one's hands, without any weapons. However, it is not simply about combat. Karate's principal objective is to unify the body with the mind and spirit. Those who study karate need to reflect on these two fundamentals: "Karate begins and ends with respect" and "There is no first attack in karate."

KARATEKA

A person who begins and continues the study of karate under the guidance of a *sensei*.

LESSONS

A normal karate training session begins with warm-up exercises. Then the class will do:

- *Kihon*, or basic movements
- *Kata*, or a series of moves done in a precise order that represent fighting against more than one opponent
- *Kumite*, or fighting against one's opponent. It literally means "meeting" (*kumi*) of "hands" (*te*), and it is understood to mean sparring. The goal is for the student to face his or her own limits and fears.

The session ends with cool-down exercises.

NUMBERS

1 - ICHI	6 - ROKU	
2 - NI	7 - SHICHI	
3 - SAN	8 - HACHI	
4 - SHI	9 - KYU	
5 - GO	10 - JU	

In class, the teacher often counts in Japanese.

OSU!

Osu is used as a general greeting among karate students. It is a combination of two words: *oshi*, which means "push," and *shinobu*, which means "endure." It implies patience, determination, appreciation, respect, and perseverance.

RESPECT

Respect is the first thing karate students learn. This includes respect for yourself, respect for your fellow students, respect for the opponent who is facing you, respect for your *sensei*, and respect for the *senseis* of the past.

SENSEI

A person who teaches karate. The master deserves absolute respect from his or her students.

UKE

A block. This skill allows you to block any attack coming to your face or body. There are six basic kinds of *uke*: upward, downward, from the outside in, from the inside out, straight, and circular.

ZUKI

Zuki is the word for a punch done with a closed hand (fist). It's usually paired with another word to describe the type of punch.

HOW TO BECOME A
CHAMPION

1 **ALWAYS TRY TO FOLLOW *DOJO KUN* RULES** inside and outside your classroom. If you do, you'll always feel good about yourself.

2 **KEEP ON PRACTICING,** even when you don't feel like going to the *dojo*. Afterward, you'll be glad you did.

3 **ALWAYS FOLLOW YOUR *SENSEI'S* INSTRUCTIONS.** Remember he or she is there to help you!

4 **DON'T EVER GIVE UP.** Karate is a practice that requires time and patience.

5 **IF YOU HAVE ANY PROBLEMS, TALK ABOUT THEM WITH YOUR *SENSEI*.** He or she will be able to give you advice.

6 **START BY ENTERING A TOURNAMENT.** If you like it, then you can continue. If you don't, take a break and try it again later on. The nice thing about karate is that it's not just about competition. You practice karate for yourself.

7 When you leave for a tournament, **ALWAYS BRING SOME FOOD WITH YOU,** like crackers, fruit, or water. You never know what kind of food you'll find there.

8 Before training, **EAT A DISH OF PASTA.** It will give you the energy you need. In the evening, eat foods rich in protein, like meat or beans, to rebuild your muscles.

9 **ALWAYS STRETCH** before and after training. It will help you warm up your muscles so you won't get hurt. It's important to keep your muscles loose and elastic.

10 **BE SERIOUS ABOUT YOUR TRAINING,** but remember to have fun, too!

karate trivia

Island of Okinawa

Okinawa

The Origins. Because of Okinawa's vulnerable position, it was invaded many times. The inhabitants had their own form of martial arts — using an empty hand. So when weapons were banned in the mid-fifteenth century, the people of Okinawa were able to protect themselves using the empty-hand (*kara* = empty; *te* = hand) technique.

The First School. Nineteenth-century karate master Sokon Matsumura's teachings tell of three methods of fighting: the technique of an empty hand; the Japanese art of the sword; and the Chinese art of fighting. All modern karate derives from Matsumura's teachings.

Modern Karate. In 1901, Anko Itosu introduced the teaching of karate into schools, thus transforming the practice of karate from individual training to group training.

Gichin Funakoshi officially introduced the practice of karate to Japan in 1922. In 1938, his students founded the first *dojo*, *Shotokan*, which means "The House of the Sound of Wind in the Pines." *Shoto* was Funakoshi's pen name.

A picture of Sensei *Funakoshi hangs in many* dojos.

Want to read my next adventure?
I can't wait to tell you all about it!

MIGHTY MOUNT KILIMANJARO

Rat-munching rattlesnakes! I can't believe it. I just let my super-sporty friend Bruce Hyena convince me to go on another one of his extreme adventures. You know me . . . I just can't say no to a friend! This time, we're going to be climbing to the top of the famouse Mount Kilimanjaro in Africa. Moldy mozzarella! I'm in no shape for a mountain climb. How will I ever make it to the top?

If you like my brother's books, check out the next adventure of the Thea Sisters!

THEA STILTON AND THE GHOST OF THE SHIPWRECK

There's a haunted shipwreck off Whale Island, and a rare diamond was lost when the ship sank. When the Thea Sisters' biology professor disappears, the mice have to dive deep into the ocean to find him— and hopefully recover the priceless jewel! And just when they think their adventures are over, the five mice are invited to China to search for another lost treasure!

Be sure to check out these other exciting Thea Sisters adventures:

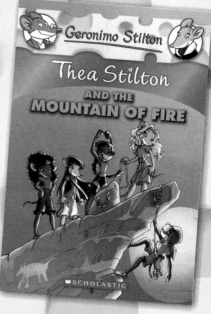

Listen to a Double Dose of Geronimo's "Fabumouse" Adventures on Audio!

MORE 2-AUDIOBOOK PACKS AVAILABLE NOW:

WRITTEN BY *Geronimo Stilton*   READ BY *Bill Lobley*

■SCHOLASTIC
AUDIOBOOKS
www.scholastic.com/geronimo

And don't miss any of my other fabumouse adventures!

#1 LOST TREASURE OF THE EMERALD EYE

#2 THE CURSE OF THE CHEESE PYRAMID

#3 CAT AND MOUSE IN A HAUNTED HOUSE

#4 I'M TOO FOND OF MY FUR!

#5 FOUR MICE DEEP IN THE JUNGLE

#6 PAWS OFF, CHEDDARFACE!

#7 RED PIZZAS FOR A BLUE COUNT

#8 ATTACK OF THE BANDIT CATS

#9 A FABUMOUSE VACATION FOR GERONIMO

#10 ALL BECAUSE OF A CUP OF COFFEE

#11 IT'S HALLOWEEN, YOU 'FRAIDY MOUSE!

#12 MERRY CHRISTMAS, GERONIMO!

#13 THE PHANTOM OF THE SUBWAY

#14 THE TEMPLE OF THE RUBY OF FIRE

#15 THE MONA MOUSA CODE

#16 A CHEESE-COLORED CAMPER

#17 WATCH YOUR WHISKERS, STILTON!

#18 SHIPWRECK ON THE PIRATE ISLANDS

#19 MY NAME IS STILTON, GERONIMO STILTON

#20 SURF'S UP, GERONIMO!

#21 THE WILD, WILD WEST

#22 THE SECRET OF CACKLEFUR CASTLE

A CHRISTMAS TALE

#23 VALENTINE'S DAY DISASTER

#24 FIELD TRIP TO NIAGARA FALLS

#25 THE SEARCH FOR SUNKEN TREASURE

#26 THE MUMMY WITH NO NAME

#27 THE CHRISTMAS TOY FACTORY

#28 WEDDING CRASHER

#29 DOWN AND OUT DOWN UNDER

#30 THE MOUSE ISLAND MARATHON

#31 THE MYSTERIOUS CHEESE THIEF

CHRISTMAS CATASTROPHE

#32 VALLEY OF THE GIANT SKELETONS

#33 GERONIMO AND THE GOLD MEDAL MYSTERY

#34 GERONIMO STILTON, SECRET AGENT

#35 A VERY MERRY CHRISTMAS

#36 GERONIMO'S VALENTINE

#37 THE RACE ACROSS AMERICA

#38 A FABUMOUSE SCHOOL ADVENTURE

#39 SINGING SENSATION

#40 THE KARATE MOUSE

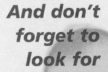

And don't forget to look for

#41 MIGHTY MOUNT KILIMANJARO

ABOUT THE AUTHOR

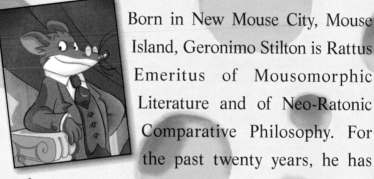 Born in New Mouse City, Mouse Island, Geronimo Stilton is Rattus Emeritus of Mousomorphic Literature and of Neo-Ratonic Comparative Philosophy. For the past twenty years, he has been running *The Rodent's Gazette*, New Mouse City's most widely read daily newspaper.

Stilton was awarded the Ratitzer Prize for his scoops on *The Curse of the Cheese Pyramid* and *The Search for Sunken Treasure*. He has also received the Andersen 2000 Prize for Personality of the Year. One of his bestsellers won the 2002 eBook Award for world's best ratlings' electronic book. His works have been published all over the globe.

In his spare time, Mr. Stilton collects antique cheese rinds and plays golf. But what he most enjoys is telling stories to his nephew Benjamin.

THE RODENT'S GAZETTE

1. **Main entrance**
2. **Printing presses (where the books and newspaper are printed)**
3. **Accounts department**
4. **Editorial room (where the editors, illustrators, and designers work)**
5. **Geronimo Stilton's office**
6. **Storage space for Geronimo's books**

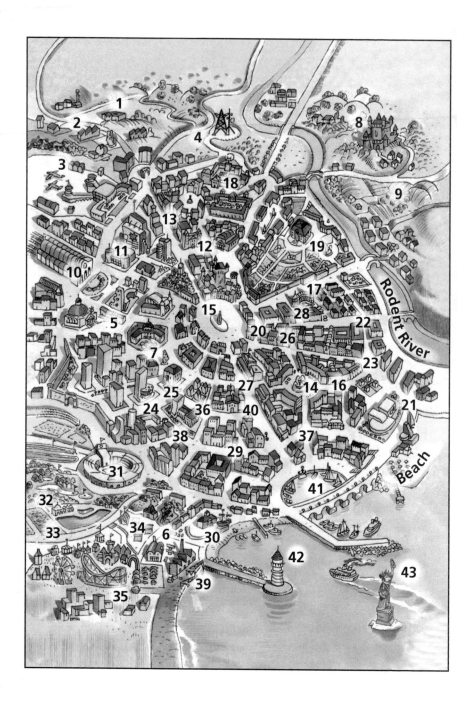

Map of New Mouse City

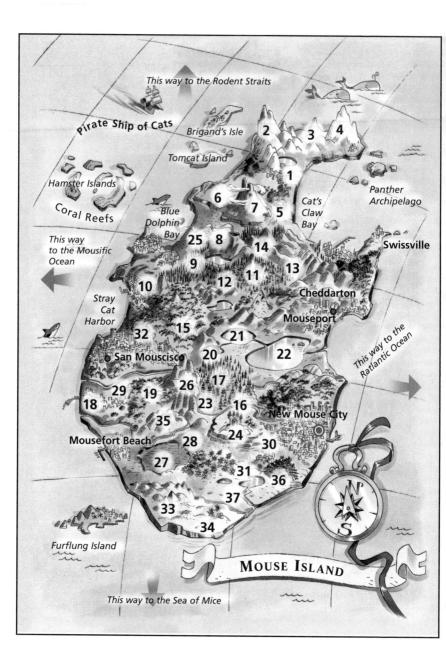

Map of Mouse Island

1. Big Ice Lake
2. Frozen Fur Peak
3. Slipperyslopes Glacier
4. Coldcreeps Peak
5. Ratzikistan
6. Transratania
7. Mount Vamp
8. Roastedrat Volcano
9. Brimstone Lake
10. Poopedcat Pass
11. Stinko Peak
12. Dark Forest
13. Vain Vampires Valley
14. Goose Bumps Gorge
15. The Shadow Line Pass
16. Penny Pincher Castle
17. Nature Reserve Park
18. Las Ratayas Marinas
19. Fossil Forest
20. Lake Lake

21. Lake Lakelake
22. Lake Lakelakelake
23. Cheddar Crag
24. Cannycat Castle
25. Valley of the Giant Sequoia
26. Cheddar Springs
27. Sulfurous Swamp
28. Old Reliable Geyser
29. Vole Vale
30. Ravingrat Ravine
31. Gnat Marshes
32. Munster Highlands
33. Mousehara Desert
34. Oasis of the Sweaty Camel
35. Cabbagehead Hill
36. Rattytrap Jungle
37. Rio Mosquito

Dear mouse friends,
Thanks for reading, and farewell
till the next book.
It'll be another whisker-licking-good
adventure, and that's a promise!

Geronimo Stilton